Paradox

By Ron Bodin

ISBN: 978-1-963239-1-88 (Paperback)

Published by **American Book Publisher**

For inquiries,

Email: ronbodin39@gmail.com

Phone: (929)-563-6133

Website: www.americanbookpublisher.com

Section 1 (Poetry)

PARADOX

By **Ron Bodin**

I stopped judging people

When I realized

That the best of people

Are capable of the worst of things,

And the worst of people

Are capable of the best of things

Awakened

By the sun

Trying to enter my cozy bedroom

Thru my mostly closed blinds

I Saw the Light!

Dog at my side

God at my back

Family intact

Writing words I love

To a life I adore

Life is good

Even thru the cracks

Of light

That I wake too few times

To See

YOUTH

Neighbors sitting on their porches Sharing stories in the
Summer heat. Wednesday smell of fresh bread baking,
Good Eating.

Mom cleaning,

Dad working board roads.

My sister and I

Learning the 3 R's,

Walking home from school,

Skipping along

Past the cemetery.

Play til nightfall,

Ronnie, Debbie, time to come home.

Rainy days

Dirt roads

Open sewerage ditches

Muck Never killed our play

Hose washed.

Hot nights meant

Sleeping near open screened doors and

windows.

Youth.

We knew we were loved.

And we knew we loved family.

Youth

I miss you.

I miss my folks,

My 21 aunts and uncles.

I miss jumping sewerage ditches.

I miss it all.

My youth.

1973

Il était une fois...

Je l'ai entendu dire trop de fois,

Mais il était une fois

Il nous a dit qu'il était gay, Nous avons compris.

Ses parents

J'aurais aimé qu'il ne soit jamais né.

Il s'est envolé vers son lieu sûr, J'ai pris un bain tiède

Lui couper les poignets

Il est mort seul, sur-le-champ. Il volait

Il était une fois

Trop de fois

Don't Forget Our Young Men

Took a personal day

Got a sub

R and R

Returned.

Note on my desk

Detailing his plan

To kill 3 staff

Named them

The when

The where

The how.

Turned it in

Not a joke.

A Young man's

Rage

Rages

He didn't know why

WRITING BY RON BODIN

Ode to my Cajun ancestors, bold and free,
Whose spirits dance upon the bayou's edge.
In your blood, the essence of history.
A vibrant tapestry, a heritage.

From Acadia's shores, you were displaced,
Yet resilience flowed within your veins,
Through swamps and marshes, you found your own space.
Creating a culture that still remains.

With gumbo simmering, a savory delight,
And zydeco rhythms, feet tapping in time,
You embraced life's pleasures, day and night,
Celebrating with laughter, a joyful chime.

Your language, a melody, unique and pure,
A blend of French and Creole, a Cajun song,
Preserving traditions, forever endure,
A legacy cherished, forever strong.
Oh, Cajun ancestors, I honor thee,
For the strength and spirit you did bestow,
In my heart, your flame will always be,
A reminder of the roots that continue to grow.

THE SUN RISES IN THE EAST

The Sun rises in the East, And the sun sets in the West.
Standing on the Equator Was standing in North And in
South.
I stood mesmerized. Volcanoes surround me Craters open
my thinking.
North

South

East

West

Good and Bad
The lamb and the tiger The dog and the swan 6am every
morning, 6pm every evening
I made peace With Myself,
With my world
In a crater near the equator The fog rolled in
Erasing Me
I am no more
In a crater on the equator!

Disguised

Life was nice
Until life wasn't.
Life was sane
Until sanity evaporated
Like a summer highway vapor.
Confused life for rain ahead,
But was never able to get to the rain.
Optical illusion.
Hit me hard
Scared me big!
Wasn't real. Wasn't right.

(Chorus)
So here's a song of thanks I sing,
For all the blessings that life brings.
For every sunrise, every gentle breeze,
For love and laughter, I'm on my knees.

(Outro)
So let us remember, each and every day,
To count our blessings, in our own special way.
For gratitude is the key, to a heart that's light,
Let's sing this song of thanks, with all our might.

(Chorus)
So here's a song of thanks I sing,
For all the blessings that life brings.
For every sunrise, every gentle breeze,
For love and laughter, I'm on my knees.

(Bridge)
In moments of darkness, when hope seems lost,
I find strength in the lessons life has taught.
For every challenge, every hurdle I've faced,

I'm grateful for the growth, the strength I've embraced.

(Verse 3)
For the beauty of nature, the wonders untold,
For the stars that shine, and the moon's gentle glow.
For the sun that warms, and the rain that falls,
For the miracles around us, bigand small.

Then a shooting star streaks, leaving no scars,
Coincidence whispers, "Dreams are worth more."

In these little miracles, we daily embrace,
Coincidence reveals its divine disguise,
God's hand at work, with love and grace,
Anonymously acting, before our very eyes.

For coincidence is but God's subtle art,
A reminder of his presence, ever near,
In the symphony of life, he plays his part,
Anonymously, with love, he steers.

So let us cherish these moments, so rare,
The little miracles that grace our days.

I HAD NEVER SEEN A SUNRISE

I had never seen a sunrise

Until

My daily drives to New Orleans on highway 90

When I saw the sky light up

It was spectacular!

Cajun talk and music on the radio

Smiling ear to ear

Losing sight only when I got to Paradise

I made it to paradise

Then a fork in the road

I took the one most traveled The sunrise made me do it!

MY CALIFORNIA FRIENDS

. . .

My California friends

Drove me to Baker Beach to hike To view the Golden Gate

Bridge But I couldn't get my eyes away From the older man

Stark naked

Digging a hole w shovel

On the beach for an hour

Confusion reigned

Until I saw the purpose of it all

He gave a shit!

CAJUN BOYS

Driving down 14 on a hot August afternoon

My dad's '65 Ford Custom caught a flat

No jack in the trunk

Cars whizzed by; no eye contact

Til a middle aged black gentleman stopped and offered to help

We just need a Jack

Mr. Ran

I'll change the tire

I'll pay you. He smiled. No Way

Later I had to ask

Dad, why did he stop and help?

Ronnie, he stopped to help cause he knows what it's like

(Ain't that the truth)

RUMBLE

One shy beyond belief,

The other hurt

And divorced,

Met at Mike's.

One dance led

To another. Hungry souls Kindred spirits. Went for a ride I'm his
Model T.

Down a lonely road, Car engine running, Radio humming,

Dancing on the roadway, Til daybreak.

Way to shoot

Your best shot

JOY RIDE

She couldn't cry
I didn't try.
Angry words spoken
Are hard to take back,
Fog seemed everywhere
Lost in the headlights
Moving fast
Too fast.
Pillars or Trees
Focus! Hit the gas
Airborne and ecstatic
Thunder Struck
Shoes flew
A trail of blood and guts
It's Done
"What have I done?"
White light and reels.

ONCE UPON A TIME

Once upon a time...

I've heard it said way too many times,

But once upon a time

He told us he was gay,

We understood.

His parents
Wished he'd never been born.

He flew to his safe place,

Drew a tepid bath

Cut his wrists

Died alone, then and there.

He flew

Once upon a time

Too many times.

Section 2
(Short Stories)

EDLAY T

She commenced packing. The process as usual, was deliberate, each item selected carefully and as carefully, almost tenderly, always thoughtfully. Edlay folded and put aside on the nearby bed, those items of clothing deemed suitable for the trip. The large gray suitcase was the center of attention. Each member of Edlay T's family contributed a piece of her clothing for the journey and placed them in the suitcase. Edlay inspected each piece and chose carefully. She caught sight of the activity as she looked into the mirrored closet door beside the mobile home bed. Now satisfied, she shut the valise uttering a few words some in stroke slurred, broken-English, many in Cajun.

The packing done, Edlay T walked to the mirror, her right leg pulled along, looked once, noticed her elastic looking face. At exactly five in the afternoon, Edlay T, her husband, her two children and her son in law, packed themselves into a 63 Olds.

With a wink, Edlay T ordered the trip to begin.

No one spoke; no words seemed necessary. The two hundred mile trip to the red clay hills of North Louisiana was another ordeal to be dealt with.

As the car spilt the landscape in two, the five passengers, resembling five ghosts, turned their heads almost as one, left then right, looking at landmarks set on each side of Highway 14, like pictures flashing from a far away projector, lightening up far away screens, highlighting moss-laden oak trees, slow-moving bayou algae, a straight line of whitewashed houses hoisted on pilings three feet high and a colorful road sign welcoming travelers to

Abbeville, scenes permanently etched in each traveler's mind eye.

Edlay T was first to catch sight of the church, situated on the right side the road, some three hundred feet straight ahead.

Edlay looked up at the cross topping the church steeple. Her husband crossed himself. The driver lowered his head in reverence. The two other passengers looked straight ahead.

It was just another car trip, understandably necessary, and perhaps - a pressing health matter; just another car ride to a larger city and larger hospital care. I reached over and switched on the radio. Mom's face beemed.

The family shared anecdotes over the sound of the music.

The time dad was locked in Tante Dits garage on a hot summer day by two naughty children, the trip to Canada when all went wrong and the five way farers were stranded for two days with a broken 63 olds and only enough money for either six donuts or a pack of cigarettes. Edlay T got her cigarettes. She always won at life: Everyone in the Olds nodded approval.

The music blasted as the car sped towards Lafayette, The Cajun capital.

The college educated driver laughed silently. Lafoyette represented everything to some – oil, new riches, Cajun delicacies lovingly served up to the new swarm of avaricious Americans.

Where was the capital building? A capital city needs a symbol.

Edlay T saw an empty beer can at the side of an open ditch.

A symbol is a symbol is a symbol.

Edlay T shook her head to clear it, not belonging, yet not remembering where she belonged. She knew she did not belong in the swamps and marshes with mosquitos for bodyguards.

"You can stop this car and let me out!" She meant business.

Every passenger's attention now focused on her remarks.
Edlay T winked and brushed her hair back.
We were stunned.
"Stop and let me use the toilet".
Her mischief broke the tension. The group quickly relaxed, yawned and walked, providing our mommy some private time.
The group slowly migrated back to the Olds. The passengers in place, the trip resumed. Edlay's husband, our dad, resumed his near complete silence for the next miles of the journey.

Tired, "I have had enough,". I vented, What kind of country is this? If you are rich, you live. If you are poor, you die quiet.

Edlay heard my rant, but seldom listened to angry remarks. Angry words haunted her since a teacher rebuked her use of Cajun French on the school campus. Eve never returned to her school after her third grade of RRR.
She still feel stupid, even now, fifty years later, feeling obliged to speak English to her family member.
"Are we in sherepor yet?" Mom blurting words to free herself and her past.
Three hours from home and a hundred mile from their destination, rain slowed the car's progress, and lulled by the pitter patter of a light Louisiana rain, the car's passengers, one by one, had become silent as they listened

to the repetitious tinkling splatter, watching the tiny rain drops fall, move up, and then off each window pane.
In the distance, lightening could be seen but no not heard. October 6 1981 would not soon be forgotten.
This time of reflection allowed Edlay T. Recalling her frightening past on the Coulee Kenney.

"Edlay (my grandmother's tone serious) get your sisters and brother together. Work on the backdoor and meet mama on the railroad track in front of Hebert's grocery." Edlay T's trip to her youth resumed.

"Mama, whose those men" she listened intently for a response.

"We got no liquor in the house. I don't care what my husband told you. He has not been here for a year. If he took your money for liquor, you settle that with him. I got six children to care for"

Edlay T clutched her younger sister. Her brother Roy rounded up the remaining siblings. The family ran the 2 mile rail track to Hebert Grocery. They survived. Edlay survived: The family survived her father's alcoholism and two paid to kill strangers.

Thunder awakened the passengers. Mom feared thunder and lightening.

Each lightning bolt cast a dim light on mommy. We saw the fear in her eyes, the light of the sky displayed the scar on mom's chest and the knife wound on her neck. I was brought to tears.

Edlay T was ten when first hospitalized with lock jaw. 10 surgeries followed.

Away from home for the first time in her short life mom was grateful for Huey Long for charity hospitals. Edlay T felt human engrossed by her sisters of charity who staffed the hospital. The nuns cared for her, taught her, loved their little Edlay, spoke of distant lands and curious ideas. She could be a nun. She could be anything, they insisted!

She listened, their warm smiles made her six-month
hospital confinement an experience she'd never forget.
Edlay T looked about the car. She was determined to
continue her journey alone.

She recalled her homecoming from Charity Hospital. Her
drunken father was waiting at the homestead gate, wide
eyed and slobbering, jealous of her new clothes, angry for
her missing cotton picking season and anxious to erase
crazy dreams of nunnery from her mind.

"Dey cut you ten times. Knife to Edlay's cleavage. I will
cut you once and done"

Eva looked him squarely, "What? You gonna kill me?" He
walked away shaken, perplexed and small.

Edlay T married at 18 to make room for new siblings.
Unfortunately, her newly wed husband was physically
abusive.

Her priest, her parents looked down on divorce.

Edlay T was firm. "If he hit me once, he will hurt me
again"

She left, cleaned homes, met my dad in a marriage of 40
years marked by peace, love and the birth of two children.

She survived.

Small talk increased as the group approached Shreveport.
King Drive, minutes away from the hospital. Edlay T
viewed the directional signs she could not read.

"Son, I wish I could read"

"Mom, you are a wonderful mother"

You read our needs, our wants, our mood and our life
stories"

Edlay T seemed at peace.

The 63 Olds turned into the hospital's emergency entrance
and one-by-one each family member emerged, tired, but
serene, a peace that come from believing you are in a safe
place, back in the womb, surrounded by learned healers.

Edlay T without looking back, walked down a lonely corridor. Turning right, she entered a waiting room crammed with the sick..

She saw people squatting, backs to the wall, one man laid out on a stretcher, filth all around. She wondered if she'd made the correct turn.

Edlay T headed for the nurses station, announced her presence and walked past a dozen exam rooms. She stopped at exam room 5 and made herself at home.

The nurse on duty, red with anger, marched towards Edlay T.

"M'am' I can't understand what you're saying but you must wait with others. Edlay smiled. She had a difficult time understanding the nurses clear, grammatically correct English"

Throwing back her head. The nurse exited, muttering some technical terms about it not been her problem who was where in this hell-hole of a hospital.

I could not help a retort. "Perhaps, it is your business to remove the dead body on guerney from the central waiting room"

Ain't that the truth?

Preparing herself for the inevitable exam, Edlay T lounged on the treatment table. Momentarily, closing her eyes, half awaiting another memory's intrusive entry. She squared her shoulders and waited.

Soon, two resident physicians on duty walked into the treatment room 5.

Edlay was first to pose a question. "Doc, you gonna kill me?"

"Mrs. B don't say that. They shook in their shoes.

The exam started. Age, height, address, surgical history. Edlay wondered if she'd die before the checklist was completed.

Both physicians, in unison, put down their charts, and after glancing at each other, asked the inevitable. "What seems to be the problem?"

Now sitting erect and glaring into the doctor's eyes, and long prepared for this opportunity. Edlay replied, "I am sick"

Both residents, got to work. They scanned her, thumped her, weighed her, pulsed her, blood pressurized her and decided on a treatment regimen tailored to meet Edlay's medical needs and designed to potentially save her life.

Edlay T smiled. "Blood thinners and a week's hospital stay seemed reasonable. The residents seemed relieved".

Frantically searching, The family finally found mommy and quietly, walked into the treatment room. Both residents smiled and gave a nod that all was OK.

Mom looked at me, winked and told me return to work down in Lafourche Parish.

"The lil Americans know what's best for me and I know what's best for them.

I understood her mischief.

Edlay seemed tired, but a blush came over her face as she looked at the four objects of her affection. She winked, I understood"

Edlay T never again looked back. She would not die at the hands of a teacher. She did not die at the hands of a drunk. She did not die to assassins. She certainly would not die in Shreveport.

The trip was my graduate degree in Wisdom.

Strokes can't break bonds. Strokes can't kill a Cajun woman unless she chooses to die.

She'd been to hell and back. She was not returning to the worst.

Listen! You can't kill a strong woman. Neither can you kill a culture.

Try as hard as you can, you can't. You couldn't even kill Elday T from Meaux, LA

Edlay lives and so does the Cajun culture.

Edlay T lives in every Cajun. Cajun lives in

each of us.

LA PASSION

Do you have a few minutes? I need to talk to someone about the Nightmares that haunt me.

Early on October sixth, I watched my wife twice kiss her older brother on both cheeks.
The sun was slowly rising, lighting the Nile. The river that flows North but never returns.

Aisha, my wife, it's time. She agreed. I swear she shed a bloody tear. I did not.

Instead, I put away my army knife in our bedroom nightstand.

I wondered if we would ever return to this sunrise.

Once upon a time in the bustling city of Cairo, there lived a courageous woman named Aisha. Aisha was not an ordinary woman; she was a prominent figure in the Egyptian opposition, fighting for justice and freedom in a country ruled by an oppressive regime. Her unwavering determination and fearless spirit made her a beacon of hope for those who yearned for change.
Aisha's influence and popularity grew day by day, much to the dismay of the ruling government. They saw her as a threat to their power and were determined to silence her voice. However, Aisha was always one step ahead, outsmarting their every move.

One fateful day, as tensions in Egypt reached their peak, President Anwar Sadat was assassinated. Chaos and confusion engulfed the nation, and the government seized the opportunity to crack down on dissenters. Aisha knew that her life was in grave danger, and she had to act swiftly to protect herself and her cause.

With the help of her trusted allies, Aisha devised a plan to escape the clutches of the authorities. She decided to fly to New York under the guise of seeking urgent heart surgery. It was a risky move, but she knew it was her only chance to avoid arrest and continue her fight for justice.

heart raced with a mix of anxiety and determination. As the aircraft soared through the skies, she couldn't help but reflect on the sacrifices she had made and the challenges that lay ahead.

Upon landing in New York, Aisha was immediately rushed to the hospital for her supposed heart surgery. The doctors and nurses were unaware of her true identity, treating her with utmost care and professionalism. Aisha's heart, however, was not the only thing being mended in that hospital room. She found solace in the support and encouragement she received from the medical staff, who admired her bravery and dedication to her cause.

Meanwhile, back in Egypt, the government was frantically searching for Aisha. They knew that her absence would only embolden the opposition, and they were determined to bring her back to face their wrath. However, Aisha's cunning plan had bought her precious time.

As Aisha recovered from her surgery, she began to strategize her next move. She knew that she couldn't stay hidden forever, and her people needed her guidance. With the help of her contacts in New York, she started organizing secret meetings and spreading awareness about the plight of the Egyptian people.

Months passed, and Aisha's health improved. She knew it was time to return to Egypt, to face the risks and continue her fight. With a heavy heart, she bid farewell to her newfound friends in New York and boarded a plane back to Cairo.

Upon her arrival, Aisha was greeted by a wave of supporters who had been eagerly awaiting her return. The news of her escape and her successful heart surgery had spread like wildfire, inspiring hope in the hearts of many. Aisha's determination had not wavered; if anything, it had grown stronger during her time away.

The government, now aware of her return, intensified their efforts to capture her. But Aisha was prepared. She had learned
valuable lessons during her time in New York, and she used that knowledge to outsmart her pursuers once again.

Aisha's return marked a turning point in the fight against oppression in Egypt. Her courage and resilience inspired countless others to join the opposition, and the government's grip on power began to loosen. Aisha's dream of a free and just Egypt was slowly becoming a reality. And so, the story of Aisha, the woman who led the Egyptian opposition and flew to New York for heart surgery on the day of Sadat's assassination to prevent arrest, became a legend. Her name echoed through the streets of Cairo, a symbol of hope and defiance. Aisha's unwavering spirit would forever be etched in the history of Egypt, reminding future generations of the power of one person's determination to bring about change

Like the Nile, we had flown north. Aisha, what have we done?
Listen! You need to know Aisha's health declined. Truths were finally whispered. She gasped for air. No crowds. No cheering. No democracy and no older brother.
Our son, she told me, refusing to look at me, was not mine. He was her older brother's and hers.
I couldn't believe what I'd heard.

Her son and her brother's assassin.
I could not think to think.
I kissed Aisha twice on both cheeks, and slit her throat with
my army knife, from ear to ear. A river of blood spread,
neck to pillow, to floor.
She would never return.

Aisha died a private death.
I shed a tear for my losses and for the images that come
and go and haunt me. Do you understand? I hope you
understand.

KID HERO

Once upon a time, in a small town called Sunnyville, there lived a young boy named Timmy. Timmy was eight years old and had a heart as big as the sun. He loved going to school, learning new things, and making friends. However, there was one thing that made Timmy's days at school a little less sunny - he was often bullied by a group of older kids.

Every day, these bullies would tease Timmy, call him names, and make him feel small. It made him sad, but he never let it break his spirit. Timmy knew that kindness was the most powerful weapon, and he always tried to be kind to everyone, even his bullies.

One sunny morning, as Timmy walked into his classroom, he noticed something strange. The usually cheerful atmosphere was filled with fear and confusion. His classmates were huddled together, whispering worriedly. Timmy'sheart sank as he saw his beloved teacher, Mrs. Thompson, sitting at her desk with tears in her eyes.

"What happened, Mrs. Thompson?" Timmy asked, his voice filled with concern.

Mrs. Thompson explained that a man had broken into the school and was causing trouble. He had even hurt her, the most loved teacher in the whole school. Timmy's heart filled with anger, but he knew he had to stay calm and think of a way to help.

Suddenly, an idea struck Timmy's mind. He remembered a secret passage that led to the principal's office. It was a hidden door behind a bookshelf that only a few students knew about. Timmy had discovered it during one of his adventures in the school library.

Without wasting a second, Timmy whispered to his classmates,

"Follow mel I know a way to keen us safe." His classmates, surprised by his bravery, quickly gathered around him.

Timmy led them through the secret passage, and they quietly made their way to the principal's office. They locked the door behind them, feeling a little safer. Timmy's classmates looked at him with admiration and gratitude. They realized that Timmy, the boy who had been bullied, was now their hero.

Meanwhile, the man continued to cause chaos in the school. He knocked over desks, broke windows, and made a lot of noise. But Timmy's classmates were safe, thanks to his quick thinking.

Just as the man was about to enter the principal's office, the sound of sirens filled the air. The police had arrived! They swiftly apprehended the intruder and made sure everyone was safe.

As the chaos settled, Timmy's classmates gathered around him, cheering and clapping. They realized that Timmy's kindness and bravery had saved them all. Even the bullies, who had once tormented Timmy, were in awe of his courage.

From that day forward, Timmy was no longer the bullied boy. He became known as the school hero, and his classmates treated him with respect and kindness. The bullies even apologized for their past actions and became Timmy's friends.

Timmy's story spread throughout the town, and he became an inspiration to children and adults alike. He showed everyone that even in the face of adversity, kindness and bravery could triumph.

And so, in the town of Sunnyville, Timmy's story became a legend

Bravery had saved them all. Even the bullies, who had once tormented Timmy, were in awe of his courage.

From that day forward, Timmy was no longer the bullied boy. He became known as the school hero, and his classmates treated him with respect and kindness. The bullies even apologized for their past actions and became Timmy's friends.

Timmy's story spread throughout the town, and he became an inspiration to children and adults alike. He showed everyone that even in the face of adversity, kindness and bravery could triumph.

And so, in the town of Sunnyville, Timmy's story became a legend, reminding everyone that heroes can come from the most unexpected places.

DREAMS DON'T DIE

Hang: (running towards her parents and grandmother) Mom! Dad! Grandma!

Khanh: (smiling) Hang, my little fisherman's daughter! How was school today?

Hang: It was good, Dad! We

learned about the history of

Vietnam. I wish I could have seen it before the war.

Khanh: (sighs) Yes, my dear. It was a beautiful place. But now, we must focus on the future.

Hang: (confused) What do you mean, Dad?

Mom: Hang, my love, we have some news. It's time for us to leave Vietnam.

Hang: (wide-eyed) Leave? But this is our home! Where are we going?

Dad: We're going to Hong Kong, and then to Long Beach, California. We have cousins waiting for us in Westminster.

Hang: (overwhelmed) But... why? What about our home, our friends?

Mom: The war is over, Hang. But things have changed. Your dad and I, we want a better life for you. A life of freedom and opportunities.

Hang: (teary-eyed) But what about Grandma? She can't come with us?

Dad: Hang, your grandmother is coming with us. We'll all be together.

Hang: (relieved) Oh, thank goodness. I can't imagine leaving her behind.

Mom: We'll be on a freighter, Hang. It's going to be a long journey. But

It's going to be a long journey. But we'll be together, and that's what

matters.

Hang: (excited) A freighter? That sounds like an adventure! Will we see dolphins and whales?

Dad: Maybe, my little fisherman. But it will be cold, especially at night. We'll have blankets to keep

us warm.

Hang: (snuggling closer to her grandmother) I don't mind the cold, as long as we're all together.

Mom: Hang, your grandmother and I have been dreaming about this journey. We dream about freedom, Sunday Mass, the Vietnamese Mall, and even college for you.

Hang: (dreamy) College? That sounds amazing! I want to learn

everything and make vou all proud.

On the freighter, Hang and her grandmother cuddle under a blanket)

Hang: Grandma, do you think our dreams will come true?

Grandma: (smiling) My dear Hang, dreams live on into eternity. As long as we believe and work hard, anything is possible.

(Hang wakes up shivering in the cold night)

Hang: Grandma, you're so

cold. Grandma?

(She covers her grandmother tenderly, realizing she has passed away)

Hang: (crying) Grandma... we were so close to Long Beach. So close to our dreams.

(She wipes her tears and takes a deep breath)

Hang: But I won't give up, Grandma. I'll make our dreams come true. I'll make you proud.

(Determined, Hang continues her journey, carrying her

grandmother's love and dreams with her)

THE 21

In the heart of Louisiana, where the bayou winds its way,
A tale of sorrow and bravery, I shall
now convey,
Of twenty-one brave souls, who faced a tragic fate,
In the depths of Belle Isle mine, where darkness lay in wait.
March the fifth, in sixty-eight, as midnight's hour drew
near, A deafening explosion shook the mine, filling hearts
with fear, The echoes of the blast, like thunder in the night,
Claimed the lives of these brave men, in a moment's
blinding light.
Among the fallen heroes, were twin uncles, Harry and
Harris, Bound by blood and kinship, their bond none could
compare to this, With hearts as strong as steel, they
ventured deep below, Toiling in the salt mine, where their
courage would soon show.

Their sacrifice, a testament, to the strength found deep
within,
In the face of danger, they stood tall, united till the end,
Their spirits now forever bound, as they ascend.
So let us raise our voices, in a ballad to the twenty-one,
To Harry, Harris, and their
comrades, whose work was never done,
May their souls find eternal peace, in the heavens high
above,
And their memory forever cherished, bound by eternal
love.
In the heart of Louisiana, where the bayou winds its way,
We'll remember these brave men, each and every day,
For their sacrifice and bravery, in the Belle Isle mine's dark
night, Shall forever be engraved, in our hearts, shining
bright.

Harry, a man of laughter, with a spirit bright and bold,
Harris, a gentle soul, with a heart of purest gold,
Side by side, they worked each day, their laughter filled the
air, But destiny had other plans, a tragedy they couldn't
bear.
The news spread like wildfire, through the towns and fields
afar, Mothers wept, fathers mourned, as they gazed upon
the stars, Wives and children left behind, their hearts
forever scarred, By the loss of their beloved, their
protectors, strong and charred.
Oh, the Belle Isle salt mine, a place of toil and sweat,
Where dreams were forged in darkness, and hope was
never met,
But amidst the sorrow and despair, a glimmer of light did
shine,

For the memory of these brave men, forever shall define.
They were fathers, sons, and brothers, pillars of their kin,
Their sacrifice, a testament, to the strength found deep
within,
In the face of danger, they stood tall, united till the end,
Their spirits now forever bound, a they ascend.
So let us raise our voices, in a ballad to the twenty-one,
To Harry, Harris, and their comrades, whose work was
never done,
May their souls find eternal peace in the heavens high
above, And their memory forever cherished, bound by
eternal love.
In the heart of Louisiana, where th bayou winds its way,
We'll remember these brave men, each and every day

MY HOMETOWN

Down in the heart of the Bayou State, lies a town called
Erath, so great,
Where the sugar cane fields kiss the southern sky, and the
crawfish dance as the day goes by.
A place of strength, a place of pride, where the spirit of
Louisiana resides,
But there's a tale of courage, we must unfold, of seven
brave men, so bold.
(Chorus)
Oh, the winds of Hilda, they did blow, across the bayou,
high and low,
Seven men stood tall, in the storm's cruel path, heroes of
our dear Erath.
They gave their lives, in the
darkest hour, a testament to Cajun power,
In the heart of the hurricane, they stood their ground, their
legacy, forever bound.

Civil Defense, their duty called, as the hurricane winds
fiercely
brawled,
They stood their ground, they did not flee, their mission to
set their people free.
Through the rain, the wind, the fear, their voices rang out,
loud and clear,
"Stay safe, stay strong, we'll see this through, for Erath,
Louisiana, we stand true."
(Chorus)
Oh, the winds of Hilda, they did rage, a fierce battle, they
did wage,
Seven men of valor, in the storm's fierce wrath, heroes of
our dear Erath.

They gave their all, in the
tempest's might, a beacon in the darkest night,
In the heart of the hurricane, they held the line, their
bravery, forever enshrined.
(Bridge)
In the face of danger, they did not hide, their courage, their
love, could not be denied,
Seven men of Erath, their story we tell, in our hearts, their
memory dwell.
(Chorus)
Oh, the winds of Hilda, they did roar, but the spirit of
Erath, it soared,
Seven men, their duty done, under the Louisiana sun.
They saved lives, in the hurricane's wrath, heroes of our
dear Erath, In the heart of the storm, they made their stand,
their sacrifice, forever grand.

HUEY'S HOMERULERS

Il était une fois, dans l'État de Louisiane, une bataille politique féroce qui faisait rage. C'était l'époque de la Grande Dépression et le peuple était désespéré de voir les choses changer. Au cœur de cette tempête se trouvait une figure charismatique et controversée, Huey P. Long.

Huey P. Long, surnommé le Kingfish, était devenu gouverneur de Louisiane. Ses politiques populistes et ses discours
enflammés lui avaient valu le cœur des classes laborieuses. Cependant, tout le monde n'était pas séduit par ses méthodes. Dudley Leblanc, un avocat et homme politique éminent, était l'un des opposants les plus virulents du régime de Long.

Leblanc pensait que les méthodes de Long étaient autocratiques et que ses promesses de

tandis que ses opposants y virent une opportunité de façonner l'avenir de l'État. Dudley Leblanc et son groupe saisirent l'instant, jurant de poursuivre leur combat contre l'héritage de Huey P. Long.

Leblanc, propulsé sur le devant de la scène, prononça un discours puissant condamnant la violence et appelant à l'unité. Il exhorta le peuple de Louisiane à se rassembler, à panser les plaies de la division et à construire un avenir meilleur. Ses paroles résonnèrent auprès de nombreux citoyens fatigués de la rivalité amère entre Long et ses opposants.

Au fil des années, Dudley Leblanc devint une figure éminente de la politique louisianaise. Il défendit des causes telles que la réforme de l'éducation, les droits des travailleurs et la justice sociale. Ses efforts contribuèrent à redistribution des richesses n'étaient que des paroles en l'air. Il voyait en Long un démagogue, utilisant son pouvoir pour manipuler les masses à des fins personnelles. Leblanc, accompagné d'un groupe de personnes partageant ses idées, forma un mouvement d'opposition pour défier l'autorité de Long.

La tension entre Long et Leblanc atteignit son paroxysme lors d'une journée fatidique à Baton Rouge, la capitale de l'État. Long avait
convoqué une session spéciale de la législature pour faire passer ses politiques controversées. Sentant l'occasion de confronter Long directement, Leblanc et ses partisans se rassemblèrent devant le bâtiment du Capitole, armés de pancartes et de détermination.

Alors que la session commençait, la voix de Long résonnait dans les

Long et ses opposants.

Au fil des années, Dudley Leblanc devint une figure éminente de la politique louisianaise. Il défendit des causes telles que la réforme de l'éducation, les droits des travailleurs et la justice sociale. Ses efforts contribuèrent à façonner une société plus inclusive et équitable, visant à élever tous ses citoyens.

L'assassinat de Huey P. Long avait à jamais changé le paysage politique de la Louisiane. Il servit de rappel brutal des dangers de l'extrémisme et de l'importance du dialogue civilisé. L'héritage de Long et de Leblanc serait à jamais lié, leurs noms gravés dans les livres d'histoire comme des symboles d'une époque
tumultueuse qui façonna l'avenir de l'État.

THE YEAR WAS 85'

In the year of '85, a journey I embarked,
To the land of my ancestors, where memories sparked,
France, the home of heritage, a tale to unfold,
A Cajun soul seeking roots, a story yet untold.
With excitement in my heart, I set foot on foreign land,
To meet our exchange student's kin, a family so grand,
Their warmth embraced me, as if I were their own,
A connection formed, a bond that had grown.
Through cobblestone streets, we wandered hand in hand,
Exploring the beauty of France, a picturesque land,
From Paris to Provence, each corner a delight,
A tapestry of culture, a vibrant, vivid sight.

But it was in Lourdes, a place of faith and grace,
Where I sought solace, in hopes to
find my place,
Amidst the pilgrims, I knelt and
closed my eyes,
Praying for guidance, a truth to realize.
Yet, as I wandered through the streets, feeling alone,
A realization struck me, like a truth carved in stone,
I am not French, I am American, Cajun to the core,
A culture rich and vibrant, one I can't ignore.
Delusions must be shed, like a veil from my eyes,
To see the world clearly, without any disguise,
For my roots run deep, in the
bayous and the swamps,
In the music and the food, in the
Cajun stamp.

So, I embraced my heritage, with a newfound pride,
No longer lost in dreams, but standing by my side,

For in that moment of clarity, I finally understood,
That being Cajun-American, is a gift, something good.
And as I bid adieu to France, my ancestral land,
I carried with me memories, like grains of golden sand,
A journey of self-discovery, a lesson to be learned,
That embracing who we are, is where true wisdom is
earned.

EYES WIDE OPENED

In tender youth, my heart did first take flight,
A love so pure, a flame that burned so bright.
Her eyes, like stars, did twinkle in the night,
And in her presence, all my fears took flight.
But as the seasons changed, so did our love,
A subtle shift, a darkness from above.
Her laughter turned to tears, her touch grew cold,
And in my heart, a story yet untold.
For love, it seemed, had turned to bitter strife,
A twisted path that led to
endless strife.
Her sweet caress, now laced with
poison's sting,
And in my soul, a sadness took its wing.

Addiction's grip, it tightened day by day,
A cruel companion, leading
me astray.
Her love, once pure, now tainted
by desire,
And in my heart, a raging, burning fire.
The drama played, a tragic tale unfold,
A love once cherished, now a story old.
I made a choice, to break the chains that bind,
And in my soul, a freedom I did find.
Forever single, I resolved to be, A world traveler, roaming
wild and free.
No longer bound by love's deceitful snare,
And in my heart, a newfound love affair.

With every step, I sought to heal my soul,
In distant lands, where

mysteries unfold.
A dog companion, loyal by my side, And in my life, a love that
can't subside.
So now I wander, free from love's cruel game,
A world traveler, with no one
to blame.
In solitude, I find my
heart's delight,
A dog lover, forever in the light.

Section 3
(Inspirational Stories)

COINCIDENCE

In the realm of life's intricate dance,
Where chance and fate intertwine, There lies a force,
unseen, perchance,
Coincidence, divine and benign.
For in each moment, a
tapestry weaves,
Threads of happenstance, delicate and fine,
God's hand at play, as the universe he conceives,
Anonymous, yet present, in every design.
A meeting of souls, in a crowded street,
Two strangers, destined to intertwine,
Their paths converge, as if by deceit,
Coincidence whispers, "This is divine."
A lost key, misplaced in haste,

Then a friend arrives, with a smile on their face,
Coincidence whispers, "Relief, you shall find."
A dream, long forgotten, buried deep,
Suddenly resurfaces, vivid and clear,
A message from the past, a memory to keep,
Coincidence whispers, "Remember, my dear."
A phone call, unexpected
and unplanned,
From a loved one, miles away, Their voice, a balm,
soothing and grand,
Coincidence whispers, "Love finds a way."
A wish, whispered softly to
the stars,
A longing, hidden within the
heart's core,

Then a shooting star streaks, leaving no scars,
Coincidence whispers, "Dreams
are worth more."
In these little miracles, we
daily embrace, Coincidence reveals its divine disguise,
God's hand at work, with love
and grace,
Anonymously acting, before our
very eyes.
For coincidence is but God's
subtle art,
A reminder of his presence,
ever near,
In the symphony of life, he plays his part,
Anonymously, with love, he steers.
So let us cherish these moments, so rare,
The little miracles that grace our days,

I THANK GOD FOR LIFE

(Verse 1)
In this world of chaos and strife,
I find solace in the rhythm of life. Through the ups and
downs, I've come to see,
The power of gratitude, it sets me free.
(Chorus)
So here's a song of thanks I sing,
For all the blessings that
life brings.
For every sunrise, every
gentle breeze,
For love and laughter, I'm on
my knees.
(Verse 2)
For the friends who've stood by
my side,
Through tears and laughter,
they've been my guide.
For family, the ones who've shaped
my soul,
Their love and support, they make me whole.

(Chorus)
So here's a song of thanks I sing,
For all the blessings that
life brings.
For every sunrise, every
gentle breeze,
For love and laughter, I'm on my knees.
(Bridge)
In moments of darkness, when hope seems lost,
I find strength in the lessons life has taught.
For every challenge, every hurdle I've faced,

I'm grateful for the growth, the strength I've embraced.
(Verse 3)
For the beauty of nature, the
wonders untold,
For the stars that shine, and the
moon's gentle glow.
For the sun that warms, and the
rain that falls,
For the miracles around us, big and small.

(Chorus)
So here's a song of thanks I sing,
For all the blessings that
life brings.
For every sunrise, every
gentle breeze,
For love and laughter, I'm on my knees.
(Outro)
So let us remember, each and every day,
To count our blessings, in our own special way.
For gratitude is the key, to a heart that's light,
Let's sing this song of thanks, with all our might.

LULLABY

Dors, mon petit bébé, Dans tes rêves enchantés, La lune brille si belle, Comme une étoile rebelle.

Les étoiles dansent dans le ciel, Comme les feux du carnaval, Les bayous chantent doucement, Pour endormir ton cœur d'enfant.

Repose-toi, mon trésor, Dans les bras de l'amour, Que la nuit t'apporte la paix, Et des rêves remplis de gaiet

MERCY GRACE

In the depths of my soul, I stand amazed,
By mercy's touch, my spirit
is raised.
For I, a sinner, deserving of blame, Was saved from
punishment, by grace's flame.
Oh, how I marvel at this wondrous gift,
That rescued me, my spirit to uplift.
For in my weakness, I found
strength anew,
As mercy's embrace, my heart did pursue.
And through the years, grace has been my guide,
Opening doors, where
opportunities reside.
Teaching jobs bestowed, a chance
to impart,
Knowledge and wisdom, to eager hearts.

Hiking volcanoes in Quito's
lofty heights,
Witnessing nature's power, in awe- struck sights.
An invitation, to the White House grand,
A moment surreal, as I took a stand.
Undeserved, yet grateful, I humbly stood,
In the presence of power, where dreams withstood.
But in this journey, I've learned a truth profound,
That mercy and grace, in
abundance abound.
And so, I'm compelled, to extend
the same,
To those who enter my life, without any claim.

For I know the feeling, of undeserved grace,
And the warmth it brings, as it lights up my space.
So, I'll show mercy, to those who
have erred,
And grace to all, for we're all undeserved.
In this dance of life, where blessings unfold,
I'll cherish each moment, as
stories are told.
Undeserved, yet grateful, my heart
shall remain,
A vessel of mercy, where grace shall sustain.

JUDGE NOT

In the realm where paradoxes thrive, Where life's mysteries
are alive, I ceased to judge, began to see, The depth of
human complexity.

The noblest hearts may falter, fall, In shadows where the
darkness calls,
Yet in their fall, they rise anew, A testament to strength so
true.

The ones we deem as less than best, In trials, they may pass
the test, Unveiling virtues, pure and bright, In darkest hour,
they bring the light.
So, let us not in judgment stand, But seek to understand
each hand, That life, in all its paradox,
Is not confined to a single box.

For every soul that walks this earth, Holds within,
immeasurable worth, In every heart, both light and shade,
In paradox, we are all made.

So, let us celebrate this dance, Of contrast, change and
circumstance,
For in this paradox we find,
The boundless tapestry of mankind.

ODE TO MY CAJUN ANCESTORS

Merci, ô Dieu, pour la culture cajun,
Un trésor précieux, un don divin.
Dans les bayous de Louisiane,
Elle brille comme une étoile sereine.

Les accents chantants, les mots en Français,
La musique joyeuse, les danses endiablées.
Les saveurs épicées, les plats délicieux,
La joie de vivre, l'amour généreux.

Les fêtes animées, les rassemblements,
Où l'on chante, où l'on danse passionnément.
Les histoires racontées, les traditions transmises,
Un héritage riche, une culture éprise.

Ode to my Cajun ancestors, bold and free,
Whose spirits dance upon the bayou's edge.
In your blood, the essence of history,
A vibrant tapestry, a heritage.

From Acadia's shores, you were displaced,
Yet resilience flowed within your veins,
Through swamps and marshes, you found your own space,
Creating a culture that still remains.

With gumbo simmering, a savory delight,
And zydeco rhythms, feet tapping in time,
You embraced life's pleasures, day and night,
Celebrating with laughter, a joyful chime.

Your language, a melody, unique and pure,

A blend of French and Creole, a Cajun song,
Preserving traditions, forever endure,
A legacy cherished, forever strong.
Oh, Cajun ancestors, I honor thee,
For the strength and spirit you did bestow,
In my heart, your flame will always be,
A reminder of the roots that continue to grow.

Merci, Dieu

"Merci, Dieu
tout-puissant,
Pour les biens que tu
nous donnes,
Pour la vie, la santé
et l'amour,
Nous te rendons grâce
ce jour-là.
Dans la joie comme
dans les épreuves,
Tu es là, guide
et soutien,
Nous te sommes
reconnaissants,
Et nous te glorifions, Ô
Dieu tout-p ant."

INK STOP STINKIN' THINKIN'

1.
In the mirror, I see a face,
A reflection of failure, a symbol of disgrace.
Solution:
But look again, with eyes anew, See strength, resilience, a
spirit true.

2.
I'm a burden, a weight, a heavy load,
A tiresome traveler on life's road. Solution:
No, you're a warrior, strong and brave,
A beacon of hope, a soul to save.

3.
I'm not enough, I'm incomplete, A puzzle missing a vital
piece. Solution:
You're a masterpiece, unique and rare,
A beautiful soul, beyond compare.

4.
I'm a mistake, a blunder, a flaw,
A creature of chaos, breaking the law.
Solution:
You're a lesson learned, a path
to grow,
A testament to strength, a beacon's glow.

5.
I'm a shadow, a ghost, unseen, A forgotten memory, a
might- have-been.
Solution:
You're a star, shining bright, A beacon in the darkest night.

6.

I'm a failure, a loser, a defeat, A player in life, who knows
only retreat.
Solution:
You're a fighter, a victor,
a champion,
A warrior who battles till the war
is won.

7.

I'm a mess, a disaster, a ruin, A ship lost at sea, in
stormy brewing.
Solution:
You're a phoenix, rising from the ash,
A symbol of hope, making a splash.

TRIBUTE TO MY MOTHER AND FATHER

I carry your love, like a precious gem,

Embedded deep within my

very core,

And as I navigate life's winding path,

Your wisdom guides me, forevermore.

So, here I stand, with gratitude

and grace,

To honor the love that you both bestowed,

In my heart, your memory will

forever dwell,

A testament to the love that

truly glowed.

George and Edlay, my beloved parents dear,

Though you are gone, your love will

never fade,

For in my heart, you'll

forever reside,

In the tapestry of memories we made.

Made in the USA
Columbia, SC
29 March 2025

55855946R00035